THE GOLDEN ARMOUR

ARACHNID
THE KING OF SPIDERS

With special thanks to Lucy Courtenay

For Sheila Noble

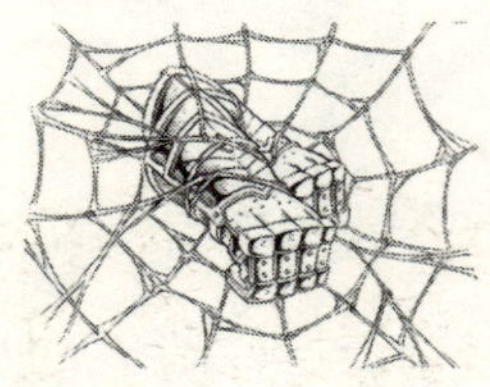

www.beastquest.co.uk

ORCHARD BOOKS
338 Euston Road, London NW1 3BH
Orchard Books Australia
Level 17/207 Kent St, Sydney, NSW 2000

A Paperback Original
First published in Great Britain in 2008

Beast Quest is a registered trademark of Beast Quest Limited
Series created by Beast Quest Limited, London

A CIP catalogue record for this book is available
from the British Library.

ISBN 978 1 84616 992 2

27 29 30 28 26

Printed and bound by CPI Group (UK) Ltd, Croydon, CR0 4YY

The paper and board used in this paperback are natural recyclable products made from wood grown in sustainable forests. The manufacturing processes conform to the environmental regulations of the country of origin.

Orchard Books is a division of Hachette Children's Books,
an Hachette Livre UK company.

www.hachette.co.uk

ARACHNID
THE KING OF SPIDERS

BY ADAM BLADE

ORCHARD

WESTERN OCEAN
THE FOREST OF FEAR
THE RUBY DESERT

Avantia
TRAL
NS
RASSY
LAINS
KING
HUGO'S
PALACE
THE CITY
ERRINEL
NG RIVER
THE DARK JUNGLE

Did you think it was over?

Did you think I would accept defeat, and disappear?

No! That can never be. I am Malvel, the Dark Wizard who strikes fear into the hearts of the people of Avantia. I still have much more to show this kingdom, and one boy in particular – Tom.

The young hero liberated the six Beasts of Avantia from my curse. But his fight is far from over. Let us see how he fares with a new Quest, one that will surely crush him and his companion, Elenna.

Avantia's Beasts had good hearts that I corrupted for my own wicked purpose. Now, thanks to Tom, they are free to protect the kingdom once more. But I have created six new supreme Beasts whose hearts are evil and so cannot be set free: monster squid, giant monkey, stone charmer, snake man, king of spiders and three-headed lion. Each one guards a piece of the most precious relic of Avantia, which I have stolen: the suit of golden armour that gives magical strengths to its rightful owner. I will stop at nothing to prevent Tom collecting the complete suit and defeating me again. This time he will not win!

Malvel

PROLOGUE

The two women stood on the rocky mountain, gazing down into the cave. It gaped below them, dark and uninviting.

"Are you really going in, Etta?" asked Dorina, the first woman.

Her friend nodded. "My father told me about this place," she said. "It's where you find the best crystals."

Dorina shivered. "I don't like it here,"

she said, glancing up at the dark forest above them. "The giant spider may be close by."

"Arachnid won't come out of the forest in daylight," said Etta, tying a rope around her waist. "We are perfectly safe."

Dorina hugged herself. "My neighbour told me there were webs in her house this morning," she said. "Great sticky ropes all over her bed. The spider's coming down the mountain looking for food. Into our village. Into our houses! Don't pretend you aren't scared."

"If the spider is real, then the crystals in these caves will protect us," said Etta firmly.

She lashed the other end of her rope to a nearby tree. Then she put a candle into a special holder and attached it to the leather cap she was wearing. With shaking hands, her friend lit the wick. Slowly, Etta lowered herself into the darkness.

"Be careful!" Dorina called after her.

The air inside the cave was musty and damp. Etta felt as if the mountain was pressing in on her, but she made herself go on. The candle in her cap flickered in the gloom. She could hear the nervous thump of her heart as she squeezed through the narrow channel of rock. The air grew colder as the cave opened up, and Etta gasped at the incredible sight before her.

The cave was like a cathedral. Huge stalactites hung from the roof and dripped icy water. Even larger stalagmites rose from the floor like church spires. Glistening blue crystals covered the walls.

"Dorina!" Etta called over her shoulder. "I've found them!"

Reaching for her pick, she began to chip at the crystals. A beautiful shard came away in her hand. Etta held it up to admire the way it sparkled in the candlelight.

Suddenly the crystal's gleam seemed to cloud. Etta peered more closely at the shard and rubbed it on her sleeve. As she frowned in confusion, she felt something damp on her shoulder. She looked up.

A long string of saliva was dripping from a set of deadly fangs that loomed high above her.

Paralysed with terror, Etta looked up into the six glittering eyes of an enormous black spider. Its swaying shadow filled the cave.

The shard of crystal fell from Etta's

hand. She opened her mouth to scream, but it was too late.

Thick ropes of silk fell on her like a net, pinning her to the rockface and smothering her. Struggling violently, Etta tried to free herself. It was no use. Faintly, she heard Dorina calling before the spider swiped at the rocks above them and brought them tumbling down, blocking the cave's entrance.

Arachnid's hideous, hairy legs moved fast, spinning and whirling the silk around his victim. Then he scuttled back to the centre of his mighty web.

Watching.

Waiting.

CHAPTER ONE

DESTINY!

Tom and Elenna watched Epos, the great flame bird of Avantia, soar into the glow of the setting sun.

"I can't believe we just rode on Epos's back," Elenna said, her eyes wide with excitement.

"Storm and Silver can't believe it, either," Tom grinned. "It's not every day that a stallion and a wolf ride on a phoenix."

Storm shook his coal-black mane and nuzzled the silver-coloured wolf at Elenna's side.

Tom removed his magical golden helmet and gazed at it with pride. He now had four pieces of Avantia's enchanted armour to help him in his Quest to save his friend Aduro, King Hugo's wizard, who had been kidnapped by the Dark Wizard, Malvel. The helmet granted Tom extra-keen sight, the chainmail gave him great strength of heart in battle, the breastplate made him physically strong and the leg armour allowed him to run fast over long distances. But there were still two pieces of armour to find, and they were protected by two more evil Beasts. Only when he and Elenna had defeated those Beasts could they vanquish Malvel and rescue Aduro.

The four friends headed back to the village from where they had started their latest Quest for supplies. Elenna handed him the flask of water for which they had bartered. Tom drank deeply. The battle they had fought against Vipero the snake man in the desert was still on his mind. It had been the toughest test Tom had ever faced. But he, Elenna, Storm and Silver had done it, and Tom had retrieved the leg armour. It was time for the next challenge.

"We have to go on," Tom said, returning the flask to Elenna.

Storm whickered gently and pushed at Tom with his nose.

"No, Tom," said Elenna, her hand resting on Silver's back. "First we must rest."

"But Aduro needs our help more

than ever!" Tom insisted. "We've got to find the next Beast!"

"You're tired," Elenna pointed out. "You need all your strength. You're no use to Aduro like this."

Tom knew his friend was right. Reluctantly, he took off the rest of the golden armour while Elenna built a fire.

Almost as soon as the sun had vanished over the horizon, a chill crept into the desert air. Tom and Elenna pitched camp beneath a slender palm tree, ate bread and cheese, and drank water from a nearby stream. Storm cropped the grass and Silver padded silently into the darkness, bringing back two rabbits.

"We'll leave first thing in the morning," said Tom, studying his enchanted map in the firelight. "The

map is showing a road that will take us away from the desert and towards the mountains, where the next piece of armour is waiting for us."

"Perfect," Elenna yawned, settling down. "Try to sleep now."

Tom gazed at the four pieces of golden armour, glowing in the light of the campfire. He noticed that several links in the chainmail were broken and it reminded him of the danger faced by Aduro.

Malvel had told Tom that every time he lost heart, the good wizard would be lowered closer to a pit of boiling tar. Shuddering, Tom remembered the vision Malvel had shown them of Aduro. His friend and protector had been bound to a chair that dangled dangerously above the gurgling, spluttering pit. He swallowed. He couldn't let Aduro down. But doubts still swarmed through his mind. Malvel had told them that the next Beast was a monstrous spider. It sounded terrifying. How could he and Elenna fight a creature like that?

Tom fidgeted on the hard desert floor, exhausted but unable to sleep. Then he sensed Storm above him. Gently the stallion snorted and blew Tom's hair away from his face. Feeling comforted, Tom closed his eyes and felt his heart lighten. He had succeeded in so many Quests already. He could surely complete another one.

Tom slept deeply. When he awoke the next morning, the sun was peeping over the horizon. He drew on his new leg armour, feeling an instant pulse of energy.

"You take Storm," he suggested to Elenna as they packed up their belongings after breakfast. "My leg armour makes me feel as if I could run for ever."

"Sounds like a good idea to me," Elenna laughed.

She climbed onto Storm's back and settled into the saddle. Then she clicked her tongue and kicked her heels. The stallion whinnied and broke into a gallop.

Wearing the leg armour, Tom found that he could easily keep up. His legs felt like giant springs. He sprinted beside Elenna and Storm, whooping with pleasure as the wind buffeted his face. Silver raced beside him, leaping and barking with delight.

More pockets of green began to appear beside the road as they left the desert behind. Soon they were crossing wide, fertile plains planted with corn. The air was fresher here, a relief after the scorching winds of the desert.

"Look, Tom!" said Elenna in delight. "An orchard!"

Gnarled apple trees groaning with fruit stood at the side of the road, near a lively stream. Tom sprang for the nearest tree, landing easily on a branch near the bottom. He reached for the apples and dropped them down to Elenna, before hopping back to the ground. The apples were crisp and cool, and juice ran down Tom and Elenna's chins as they bit into them. Storm hungrily tore fruit from the branches, while Silver bounded between the trees and rolled in the long grass.

"I never knew an apple could taste so delicious," Tom said, grinning.

Elenna laughed. "Nor did Storm!" she said. "He must have eaten twenty."

Tom felt a surge of gratitude for his three friends. They had come so far together already. With Elenna, Storm and Silver by his side, Tom felt he could fight twenty Beasts.

As he rested against the tree, Tom suddenly saw, out of the corner of his eye, the initial "T" carved into the ancient bark. He traced the letter with his fingers, his heart thumping. Could it stand for Taladon? He felt a mixture of sadness and excitement, as he always did when he thought of the father he had never met.

"Look, Elenna," he said. "T for Taladon! Perhaps he passed this way. Perhaps..." His voice trailed off.

"You'll see him one day," said Elenna, guessing instantly what was on Tom's mind.

Tom smiled at his friend. He hoped with all his heart that she was right.

He pulled his enchanted map and then his magical compass out from Storm's saddlebag and studied them carefully. He had been given the compass by his uncle, who had told him that it had once belonged to his father. The needle showed him when to step forward to meet his destiny, and when to flee impossible danger. Tom held the compass tightly, then placed it on the map, which once again came to life. Mountains rose up in miniature, rivers gleamed and tiny trees swayed in the wind. A glowing red line appeared, showing Tom the way to a town that nestled at the edge of the mountains. Right next to the town, near a rocky outcrop, a pair of minuscule golden gauntlets glittered. The next piece of armour! Tom swivelled the compass until the needle pointed towards the town.

Destiny, it read.

Tom rolled up the map and gathered his courage.

"It's time to fight a giant spider!" he said.

CHAPTER TWO

A PARTY

Tired and hungry after their long journey, Tom, Elenna, Storm and Silver came at last to the town. It was surrounded by grey, forbidding walls, the same colour as the mountains that stood behind it.

But to Tom and Elenna's surprise, throngs of people were moving through the main gates.

"I wonder what's happening here today?" Tom said, looking around.

"Market day, perhaps," Elenna said.

The smell of freshly baked bread wafted towards them. Tom's stomach rumbled. They hadn't had a good meal for several days, and the thought of food and a soft bed was very appealing.

They followed the crowds and entered the town. Coloured streamers hung merrily from the windows of houses. Flags lined the streets, rippling in the cool mountain breeze. Market traders were selling toys and trinkets, and jugglers performed on street corners. Everywhere Tom and Elenna looked there was music and laughter. People pushed and jostled, calling out to one another in cheerful voices.

The street soon opened onto a brightly decorated town square. Wooden tables and benches lined the marketplace, and the smell of hot stew filled the air.

"Come, friends!" laughed a trader, offering Tom and Elenna shiny candied apples. "Two pennies each. Long live the King!"

"Of course!" said Elenna. "It's the King's birthday. Everyone in Avantia will be celebrating."

Tom quickly found a tethering post for Storm. "Hungry, are you?" he laughed at Silver, who had pounced on a chicken drumstick that had been dropped on the ground. "I know how you feel!"

"Join us, travellers!" called out a jolly-faced man at a nearby table. "There's plenty for all who call themselves friends of King Hugo!"

Tom and Elenna settled down on a bench and helped themselves to stew and bread. Silver sat at Elenna's feet, patiently gnawing his chicken bone.

The Quest was still on Tom's mind, but he ate hungrily, watching and listening to the people around him. Although the merriment that filled the town was infectious, he noticed several uneasy faces and wondered if the townspeople were aware that an evil Beast lived so close to them.

"Do you think they know about the spider?" he asked Elenna, leaning close to her.

She shook her head. "Why should they? To most people in Avantia the Beasts are just myth."

After the meal, the tables were cleared away and games began. An archery target was set up on one side of the square, and a children's coconut shy on the other. The street entertainers were now in the middle of the marketplace, and the townspeople danced while red-faced town musicians played their instruments.

"Come and try the coconut shy," Elenna said, dragging Tom from his seat. "Look at the prizes!"

Lined up on the wooden table beside the coconut shy were numerous rows of small, bear-like creatures made of clay.

"It's Nanook!" Tom gasped, recognising the famous Beast. The last time he had seen the snow monster had been on the icy plains in the north, where he had freed her from Malvel's evil curse.

"See what I mean?" said Elenna. "These people think the Beasts of Avantia are just fairytales, fit for children's toys."

She seized three balls. Winking at Tom, she let them fly towards the coconuts one after the other.

Thump, thump, thump. Three large coconuts fell to the ground.

The crowd around the coconut shy cheered.

"That was brilliant, missus," said a small boy, watching as Elenna collected three little Nanooks from the stallholder.

"Thanks," said Elenna. "Here!" She tossed the boy one of the toys.

"Thanks!" the boy shouted happily.

Tom watched as he scampered off, clutching his prize. It had been such a long time since he had been able to play with toys, or have fun at a street festival. The Quest had taken over his life.

"You get an extra prize for knocking off three coconuts, miss," the stallholder said to Elenna.

"Do I?" Elenna said, laughing as she gave away her remaining two Nanooks to an excited little girl and her brother. "What is it?"

"A wish," said the stallholder with

a smile. "Anything you fancy. Within reason, of course."

"Well, that's easy," said Elenna, patting Silver as he frolicked around her feet. "What I wish for is a good sleep on a comfortable mattress."

"We've been travelling for a long time," Tom explained. He wondered what he would say if the stallholder asked them where they were going. Their Quest was a secret, after all.

But the man simply nodded. Then a voice came from behind them.

"I have a spare room in my house."

Tom turned to see a tall, thin woman with dark hair. She didn't return his smile.

"That would be wonderful," said Elenna. "Thank you."

"I am Dorina," the woman said. "Please come with me."

She turned and walked away, her head down. She didn't look at the entertainers or musicians they passed. Tom and Elenna glanced at each other. It was clear that Dorina was in no mood for celebrations. Tom felt a lurch in his stomach. Perhaps this was what he had been looking for – someone who knew that danger lurked.

"Your town is very welcoming," Tom said, hurrying to catch up with her. "Have you enjoyed the festivities?"

Dorina stopped. "I have lost my friend," she said. "There is nothing for me to celebrate." Tears filled her eyes. "Etta went into the mountain caves," she explained. "I was there. I watched as she..." Her voice cracked.

"What happened?" Elenna said.

"She didn't come back," Dorina

whispered, wiping the tears from her eyes. "She went in search of the crystals that protect us. But there was some kind of earthquake. Rocks fell and blocked the entrance to the caves."

Tom's skin tingled. Was this the Beast's work?

"Why do you need protection?" he asked.

"There is a giant spider living in the high forests," Dorina sniffed. "I've heard it is called Arachnid." Tom and Elenna shivered. "The blue crystals in the caves are said to protect us. But strange things are happening in our town. Huge webs are spun around the walls in the night, and food is disappearing. Don't let these festivities fool you. We are all scared. We know that when the food is gone, the spider will come for us –

and there is nothing we can do!"

Daylight was fading. A pale moon peeped out from behind the clouds, then vanished again. The mountains above the town looked vast and dark. Tom stared up at them. He could see the fringes of a great forest on the upper slopes, black and forbidding in the dusk. Somewhere among those distant trees, the Beast was waiting for Tom, guarding the fifth piece of precious golden armour. Tom knew that to protect its prize, Malvel's evil Beast would give its life.

Would Tom have to risk his own life to retrieve the golden gauntlets?

CHAPTER THREE

SPIDER IN THE NIGHT

"Come on," Elenna said, gently placing a hand on Tom's shoulder. "We need a good night's sleep if we're going to tackle Arachnid tomorrow."

Tom fetched Storm from his tethering post. They followed Dorina to her house, in a side street near the marketplace. Tom settled Storm in Dorina's stable, then followed l and Silver into the house.

The air inside smelled of beeswax and lavender. The furniture looked well polished and the windows gleamed.

"I hope you will be comfortable," said Dorina, showing them into her spare room at the back of the house.

Two fat, hay-filled mattresses sat on wooden beds, scenting the room with a clean, grassy smell. The view from the window was of the small yard and stables below. Everything was shrouded in darkness.

"I could sleep for a week," Elenna groaned, flopping onto one of the mattresses. Silver curled up underneath the bed and settled his silvery head on his paws.

"There will be supper on the table later," said Dorina. "If you wish it."

She bowed her head and left the room, softly shutting the door behind her.

Something about Dorina's story worried Tom. After fighting ten Beasts, his instincts were starting to tell him when things weren't right.

"Do you think Arachnid has got Dorina's friend?" he asked, kicking off his boots and sitting down on his mattress.

Elenna looked surprised. "The spider is supposed to live in the forest high up on the mountainside," she said. "Not in the caves near the town. Dorina said that there was a rockfall. Don't you think her friend is dead?"

"I have a feeling that Arachnid is closer than everyone thinks," said Tom grimly. "Remember what Dorina said about the webs in the town? And the way that the food disappears eve night? And yet no one ever sees this spider. It's a long way down to the town from the mountain tops. Isn't it more likely that the spider has moved closer to his source of food, and set up home in the nearby caves?"

Elenna looked uneasy. "You may be right," she said.

Tom thumped his hand on the mattress. "We have to find Arachnid," he said. "We have to defeat him and rescue Dorina's friend. Before it's too late!"

"Hmm," said Elenna sleepily. Her eyes were fluttering and closing.

Tom wanted to go straight to the caves. But watching Elenna, he remembered how little they had slept in the past few days. She was already breathing peacefully, curled up on her soft hay mattress. It wasn't fair to drag her out into the night – not now.

Tom felt too tense to sleep. Instead, he settled down beside the window. He would keep watch. If the spider came in the night, Tom would be the first to know.

Tom woke suddenly. His neck was stiff, his arms wrapped around his knees. With dismay, he realised that he had fallen asleep on the floor by the window.

The weak moon shone into the room, filling it with a soft, misty glow. Everything was still and silent. But Silver was growling softly, his eyes bright in the moonlight. Tom glanced at Elenna, still fast asleep. Then he saw a pulsing light coming from the saddlebag on the floor.

Tom stood up stiffly and reached for his bag. He pulled out the magical map. The red path showing them the way to the mountains seemed to be glowing with extra urgency. They were running out of time.

Silver was still growling. His body was tense, ready to spring.

"Shush, boy," Tom whispered. Then he noticed something strange about the moonlight. It was as if the moon was shining through a veil of some kind. With a shiver of disgust, he saw that a thick spider's web had been woven across the window.

With a mounting sense of horror, Tom gazed around the room, swivelling slowly to take it all in. Every surface was covered with gauzy webs. He backed slowly away from the window – and found himself entangled in a prison of

clammy, silken threads.

"Arghh!" Tom yelled in shock, lashing out.

Elenna sat up in bed, startled by Tom's yell. "Yuck!" she exclaimed, tearing at the thick, sticky ropes that twisted over her sheets and blankets.

"Arachnid has been here," Tom said urgently, pulling on the four pieces of golden armour. "In this room with us, Elenna! There's no time to waste. We have to leave for the mountains at once!"

He showed Elenna the map. Wide awake now, Elenna pushed her way through the sticky webs surrounding her bed.

"This is awful," she whispered, her face pale. "We have to do something."

The floor was tacky underfoot. Tom grimaced in disgust as he reached for the lamp beside his bed and lit the wick. Quietly, they tiptoed out of the bedroom, with Silver padding silently beside Elenna.

There was no light shining beneath Dorina's door as they crept past. Webs hung from the polished banisters and formed thick curtains over the walls. There was something beautiful about the way they twisted and spiralled, glistening softly in the lamplight – and yet something deadly, too. They brushed at Tom's cheeks as he and Elenna hurried down the stairs.

"I'll leave some money in thanks," said Elenna in a low voice. "I don't want Dorina to think that we left in the night like thieves."

She took two candles from the pantry, and left a small pile of coins.

"At least the townspeople are still asleep," Tom whispered to Elenna as they led Storm out of his stable. "No one needs to know about our Quest. We can leave the town and climb the mountains by daybreak."

Just then a hand grasped his shoulder. Tom cried out.

"What are you doing?" Dorina asked, her eyes wild and frightened as she pulled a thick woollen blanket around her shoulders to ward off the night chill. "Where are you going?"

"We have urgent business," Elenna said.

"The spider came in the night," Dorina whispered. "You saw its webs. We are all lost unless you find it and kill it."

Tom gasped. How did she know about their Quest?

"You are going to find it, aren't you?" Dorina said to Tom. Her eyes were huge in the moonlight. "I watched you in the town square today. You were looking for something. You are not ordinary travellers. I can see that by your armour. Please – tell me. I must know!"

Tom had to tell her the truth. "We are," he said. "We think it's in the caves. But swear that you will tell no one!"

"I swear," Dorina said fiercely. "The tunnel Etta used is blocked now, but there is another entrance to the caves further up the mountain. The path is dangerous, but keep your back to the mountainside and you will make it. And take this; it will help you."

She pushed something cold and hard into Tom's hand. It was a shard of glittering blue crystal.

"Go," she said, backing away. "And may the Beasts of Avantia be with you!"

CHAPTER FOUR

A LONG WAY DOWN

Tom examined the crystal as Storm blew softly over his shoulder. It was certainly pretty, reminding him of a sapphire.

"That's not protection," Elenna snorted, slinging the saddlebags over Storm's back. "That's jewellery."

As he put the crystal in his pocket and gave Elenna a leg-up onto Storm,

Tom had to agree with her. He had more faith in his shield and armour than in a shiny piece of blue glass.

The candles and the red glow from the map lit their way out of the town. Thick silver webs were draped everywhere. Several unwary rats and mice struggled, caught in the silken tangles. Tom tried not to think about the size of the spider that had spun them.

The road out of town was straight and well surfaced. But as they approached the bottom of the mountain, it began to change. Soon even Tom was struggling in his magical leg armour, and Storm lost his footing several times on loose shingle. Tom shifted his shield onto his back and used his hands to steady himself, skirting puddles that gleamed in the moonlight. The sky was getting lighter. Sunrise wasn't far away.

The road dwindled to a track, growing steeper with every passing minute. Tom was glad of his golden helmet. He could see the dangers underfoot as well as the mountain track that twisted ahead of them.

They reached the rocky outcrop marked on the map just as the sun broke over the horizon.

"This must be where Etta entered the caves," said Elenna, stooping down and peering into the dark hole in the mountainside. "I can see the rocks blocking the way." She shuddered. "How terrible to be trapped down there."

"The map is showing us the other entrance," said Tom, pointing at the glowing red line. They looked up the mountainside to where the path snaked out of sight.

"Is that the only way?" Elenna said in dismay.

Dorina had warned them the path was dangerous. But it looked impossibly narrow, and to the right was a sheer drop.

"We'll be fine," Tom said.

Storm tossed his head nervously. Undeterred, Tom took the stallion's reins and led him forwards.

Elenna hung back. "Tom," she said in a choked voice. "I can't do this."

Silver nuzzled Elenna's hand comfortingly.

"You and I have fought ten Beasts," said Tom. "You can walk this path, Elenna. Trust me."

Hesitantly, Elenna began to follow her friend.

They reached the point where the path wrapped itself around the edge of the mountain. There was no turning back now.

"It's a long way down," Elenna said, looking over the edge.

There was barely room for one person to pass, and in places the path had crumbled away.

"You go first. Keep your back to the mountain," Tom instructed. "You can lean into it, and use it as a support."

They took turns to move down the path. Elenna slid along with her back to the mountain, looking straight ahead. Silver picked his way behind her, as sure-footed as ever. Seizing Storm's reins, Tom clicked his tongue. "Come on, boy," he said. "We can do this!"

Tom inched along the path, leading Storm and trying not to look down.

But he felt the path disintegrating. Stones bounced away and disappeared over the edge of the mountain. He moved a little faster. More stones fell.

"The path is collapsing! Run, Tom!" Elenna shouted in front of him.

Tom ran. Storm whinnied in terror, racing close behind him. Stumbling and slipping, Tom could feel the path crumbling behind them. Could they make it before the path fell away completely?

Tom's feet suddenly met air. His heart crashed in his chest as he grabbed at the mountainside. But the stones came away in his fist. There was nothing he could do. He was going to fall!

Instinctively, he let go of Storm's reins. He could hear Elenna scream as he plunged over the edge. Then her voice was snatched away in the wind.

The mountainside was racing past in a blur. Tom wrestled with the shield strapped to his back and pulled it over his head. The magical eagle feather that was set into his shield protected him from falling. At once, he could feel himself slowing. He angled the shield so that he could float close enough to the mountainside to find something to hold on to and stop his fall.

At last his hand clasped around a spur of rock. Tom closed his eyes.

Thank goodness! he thought. Opening them again, he looked up at the path overhead. It was a stiff climb back to the others. Steadying himself with his feet, he slung his shield back over his shoulder and began to make his way upwards. The golden breastplate pulsed strength into his chest and his legs, helping him climb.

Elenna was waiting for him, tense and white-faced. She helped Tom to pull himself over the edge and back onto solid ground, where he collapsed onto a patch of scrubby grass.

"I thought you'd gone for ever!" Elenna burst out when Tom had got his breath back.

"You can't lose me that easily," Tom said with a smile.

Elenna laughed in relief. Then she looked more serious. "There's no way back," she said. "I pulled Storm across just in time. The path has completely disappeared."

It was true. Where the path had been was now a yawning chasm.

"We'll worry about that after we've defeated Arachnid," Tom said.

He thought about the golden gauntlets. Would the spider be guarding them in his web? Tom shivered but he knew that he couldn't lose heart. Only by winning all six pieces of the armour could he and Elenna save Aduro from Malvel's evil clutches.

It was now or never.

The Beast was waiting.

CHAPTER FIVE

ARACHNID'S LAIR

Tom stood at the mouth of the cave. They hadn't had to walk much further to find it. It looked narrow and gloomy. Storm shifted restlessly, sniffing the stale air within.

"Are you ready?" Tom asked Elenna over his shoulder.

"Ready as I'll ever be," she replied, stroking the top of Silver's head. She took the candles from her pack and a flint from her pocket. With a steady hand, she struck the flint and lit the wicks. Then she passed a candle to Tom.

Tom held it above his head and led the way. Storm and Silver followed, with Elenna bringing up the rear, holding the second candle. It wasn't long before they'd left the daylight behind.

The cave floor sloped sharply. Skidding on the loose stones, Tom put his hand out. The walls were slippery and sparkled dimly under his fingers. Tom realised that they were studded with blue crystals.

He could hear Storm snorting nervously and Silver whining as they descended.

A cold gust of wind suddenly blew out the candles. Even though he was wearing his magical helmet Tom could see nothing. Would they have to continue their journey in darkness?

As Tom's eyes grew used to the gloom, he stared at the walls of the tunnel in surprise. They were glowing!

"The crystals, Tom!" Elenna whispered, reaching up to touch the blue gems. "They've taken the light from our candles and are reflecting it back at us!"

They are protecting us after all, Tom thought.

The path led around a narrow corner and into a vast, echoing cave. Tom stared in amazement at the space around them. Vast stalactites hung from the roof and stalagmites grew up from the floor. The air was damp and cool, and filled with the sound of dripping water.

Tom felt a chill in his bones. He was sure the Beast was close.

He stepped further into the cave. There was a rasping hiss from somewhere in the gloom. Then something whisked through the air towards him and grasped his waist. Looking down, Tom saw a thick rope of spider silk had wrapped around him. He tried to pull against it but the thread grew tighter, constricting his breathing.

He was right. Arachnid was in the cave!

There was another hiss. A second jet of silk landed on Elenna with the same deadly accuracy.

"Help me, Tom!" Elenna screamed, struggling as Tom pulled himself free.

Silver growled angrily and seized the web with his teeth, but it only

made things worse.

"Struggling will make it tighter," said Tom, trying to remain calm. "Stay still."

Elenna stopped struggling and steadied her breathing. She instead tried to soothe her frightened wolf. Silver growled softly.

Storm tried to back out of the cave.

"It's all right, boy," said Tom, holding his reins tightly.

The stallion calmed a little, but pawed the ground with his hooves.

Elenna threw off the sticky web with difficulty. It was hard to untangle and clung to her hair and clothes.

There was another hiss, dark and deadly sounding. Tom was ready this time, leaping out of the way as another jet hurtled towards him. He looked around. Where was Arachnid?

In the darkest part of the cave, a ghastly sight met his eyes. Sitting in the middle of an enormous web that stretched right across a cavern was a gigantic spider.

Arachnid was the size of a barn. Eight hairy legs protruded from his body, waving lazily in the air. Thick saliva dripped from his long, sharp fangs and he watched Tom carefully with six evil eyes. The Beast opened his jaw and moaned. The putrid smell of dead flesh filled the air.

Silver barked ferociously as Tom tried to see what lay beneath

Arachnid's web. The cavern looked dark, bottomless and deep.

"Look beside the spider," said Elenna in a low voice.

The golden gauntlets were sitting in the heart of the web. They were the same burnished gold as the rest of Tom's enchanted armour, and were moulded in the shape of two mighty fists.

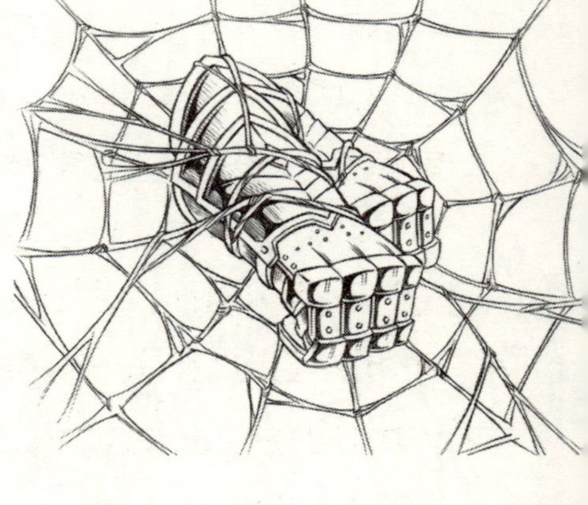

Without meaning to, Tom took a step forward. His feet crunched on something and he looked down. Scattered on the floor were piles of leathery old spider skins that Arachnid had shed. Then he realised in horror that the giant spider was drawing him in, tugging with deadly purpose on the sticky silk around his waist.

Arachnid reared back furiously. For the first time Tom saw the spider's most deadly weapons. On its underbelly were rows and rows of sharp teeth. With mounting fear, Tom saw the thigh bone of a dog in the web beside the Beast. It had been picked clean.

Tom felt himself being pulled forward again. The spider's monstrous legs were whirling, gathering in its web – and its victims.

They were going to be eaten alive!

CHAPTER SIX

THE GOLDEN GAUNTLETS

The giant spider let out another high-pitched moan that echoed off the walls of the cave. The sound chilled Tom to the bone. Then the Beast brought its long legs back down to its web. Tom felt behind him for his shield and pulled it across his body to protect him from further jets. Then he drew his sword and slashed through the web around his waist.

Thanks to his magical helmet, Tom could see every hair on Arachnid's ugly body. He could also see himself reflected in the spider's six eyes. The Beast was watching Tom's every move.

Tom readied himself for the spider's attack. But Arachnid didn't shift. He was guarding the treasure that lay in the heart of his web.

Another spurt of silk whistled towards Tom. Just in time, he lifted his shield.

Still crouched beside the gauntlets, the spider lunged at Tom with one long black leg. Tom thrust hard with his sword. The blade bounced off the spider's skin. Elenna loosed an arrow, but it clattered against Arachnid and fell uselessly into the web.

"His hide is too tough," Tom panted.

How were they going to defeat this evil Beast?

"Look up, Tom!" Elenna called. "The stalactites!"

Rows of jagged stalactites clung to the cave roof, their sharp points deadly and still dripping with the water that had formed them over thousands of years. If a stalactite fell, Tom knew that any of them could be killed instantly.

"That's it!" Tom gasped. "If I can break a stalactite from the roof,

I can use it as a spear!"

He sheathed his sword and reached for a handhold on the smooth wall. Arachnid hissed with rage as Tom began to pull himself up towards the nearest stalactite, his feet scrabbling for a foothold. It was impossible. The walls were too slippery. He fell back to the floor.

The giant spider began to move reluctantly away from the centre of its web. The gauntlets gleamed in the dim light. Tom thought of Aduro being lowered towards Malvel's deadly pit of tar. He had to get the gauntlets or die in the attempt!

Tom felt Storm push him gently with his nose. It gave him an idea. Could he use the stallion to reach a stalactite?

"Here, boy," said Tom, coaxing Storm closer to the cave wall.

Seeing what Tom was trying to do, Elenna ran to help, with Silver by her side. Tom put his foot in Storm's stirrup and Elenna gave him a leg-up on to the stallion's back. Then Tom stood on the well-worn leather saddle and reached up. His fingers brushed the rough, pointed tip of a stalactite. If he could just grasp it–

Arachnid hissed and reared again.

Storm whinnied in terror and jumped forwards, despite Elenna's best efforts to hold him still.

Tom grasped desperately at the stalactite, thrown off-balance by Storm's sudden movement. It was too late! The rock slipped from his fingers, and Tom began to fall.

There wasn't time to lift his shield above his head to protect himself. Whistling through the cold air, Tom landed on something soft. He looked beneath him and his heart thudded in his chest.

He had landed in Arachnid's web.

Tom could feel the deadly strength of the sticky fibres. He needed all the power of his magical breastplate to pull himself loose. Arachnid began to move towards him, his six eyes narrowing in pleasure. Tom struggled desperately to stay upright as the web rocked beneath him. He stretched out his hand to keep his balance, then pulled it back as the gluey ropes sucked at his fingers.

Another jet of silken thread hurtled towards Tom just as he ripped his limbs free from the web and threw himself past the spider at the golden gauntlets.

Arachnid shrieked with rage. Tom had only seconds before the Beast

attacked again. He grabbed the gauntlets and thrust his hands inside them. At once, his fingers tingled with new strength and twitched towards his scabbard. Tom instantly realised that the gauntlets would give him special skills with his sword!

He pulled the sword from its sheath. It felt like a living thing in his hands, ready to do his every bidding. The chainmail tingled around his chest, filling him with courage. With five pieces of armour and the five magical gifts they bestowed upon him, Tom knew he could defeat the spider. He whirled his sword above his head and brought it down on the silken ropes that clung to his feet.

At once, a gap opened between Tom and the Beast. But without the web, there was nothing to stop Tom from falling into the bottomless cavern beneath!

The giant spider scuttled to safety at the edge of the web as Tom fell through the hole. For the second time that day, he pulled his shield over his head, and immediately felt his fall slowing. It gave him time to reach out and

grab hold of the cavern wall.

Quickly he began to climb back up to Elenna, Storm and Silver. He had to protect them! Arachnid could attack at any moment.

His blood was thundering in his ears as he hauled himself up. His legs were still weak after his climb from the fallen path, and he knew that his armour was helping him to make the ascent. His breastplate gave him the strength he needed to pull himself upwards. His legs, encased in their special armour, pushed him steadily on. He could feel his strength and purpose returning as the magical golden armour of Avantia wrapped its protection around him. His friends were waiting for him. He wouldn't let them down!

Elenna looked over the edge of the

cavern as Tom pulled himself to the top.

Behind Elenna, Tom saw Silver. And behind Silver, the shadow of the spider was looming, its fangs dripping.

CHAPTER SEVEN

THE BATTLE BEGINS

"Silver!" Tom cried.

Elenna whirled around. But it was too late. Arachnid had pulled the wolf into his web. Silver struggled, but he was trapped.

"No!" Elenna shouted.

Arachnid's legs reached for the wolf. Silver snarled up at the giant spider. He bared his sharp teeth and swiped at the Beast with his claws. But Arachnid ignored him. Rapidly he began to spin ropes of silvery thread, wrapping the wolf up like a parcel. Growling and snapping, Silver fought back. But his struggles made things worse as the web wound more tightly around him. It was no use. He couldn't free himself.

Tom felt a surge of anger. He couldn't let Silver lose his life! Then he remembered the stalactites. He ran to the edge of the cave, his leg armour throbbing with magical energy. He leapt up and onto the wall. This time the gauntlets gave him extra grip as he hauled himself up towards the stalactites. He moved across the cave wall, foothold by foothold. Then he stretched himself as far as he could. A deadly-looking stalactite was almost within reach!

By now Arachnid had almost finished his vile work. Thick threads were wound around Silver's body. The wolf's growls and snarls were growing fainter.

"Quickly, Tom!" Elenna cried, her voice cracking. She was kneeling at

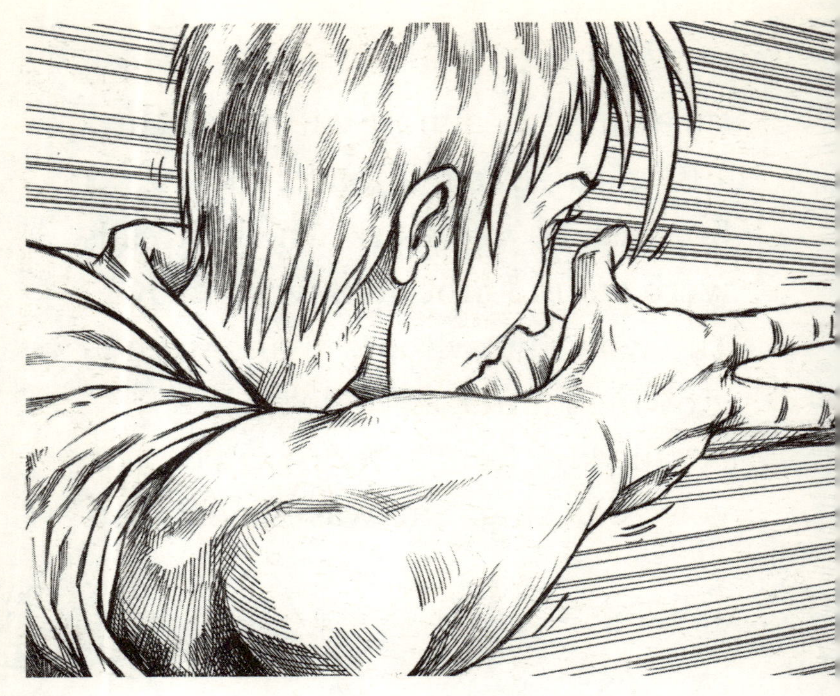

the edge of the web, reaching helplessly towards her wolf. "I don't think Silver can last much longer!" In despair, she pulled an arrow from her quiver and loosed it at the spider. It clattered uselessly away again.

Tom moved further up the wall until his head touched the cave roof. He was holding on by his fingertips. How could he continue? The armour was

giving him magical skills, but it was also heavy, dragging his body down.

Then Tom felt the breastplate fill him with fresh energy and the chainmail give him strength of heart. He could not fail! Grunting with the effort, he gripped the wall with one hand and reached for his sword. It slid swiftly from its scabbard. He swiped fiercely at the root of the stalactite. The jagged rock shuddered, but didn't come away.

Even with the magical skills of the gauntlets, Tom found it difficult to aim his sword at the right angle from his position near the roof. He twisted his body, reaching his arm as far as he could. His muscles were screaming in agony. Again and again he hacked at the stalactite. Sweat ran into his eyes, making it difficult to see.

Down below, he could just make out Arachnid toying with Silver, patting him back and forth across the web. It wouldn't be long before the Beast grew tired of his game…

Then Elenna screamed, "Look!"

Tom peered into the far corner of the cave. Something else was trussed up in the web. Something that was moaning and wriggling.

It came to Tom in a flash. Etta, Dorina's friend!

"We're coming, Etta!" Tom shouted. He hacked again at the stalactite.

"Don't give up hope!"

The wolf had stopped fighting now. He lay still at Arachnid's feet.

"Silver!" Elenna cried out, as Storm snorted and tossed his long black mane. "Oh, Silver, hold on!"

Arachnid hissed. The venom on his fangs gleamed. Tom hesitated. Both Silver and Etta needed his help! But there was so little time.

Even with his five pieces of magical armour, Tom knew that he couldn't do this on his own. It was time to call upon one of the good Beasts of Avantia. Who might be able to help?

Then the answer came to him: Nanook.

The last time Tom had seen the great snow monster was on the edge of the icy northern plains. He could only hope that the Beast would come to his aid now.

Sheathing his sword, Tom continued to grip onto the cave wall and reached around his back to touch Nanook's enchanted bell, which was set deep into his shield.

Almost instantly, he heard a mighty roar.

The Beast had come!

CHAPTER EIGHT

NANOOK TO THE RESCUE

Part of the cave wall came crashing down, revealing dazzling daylight as the snow monster thundered inside. The ground trembled.

"Nanook!" Tom cried in relief.

Seizing Storm's reins, Elenna ran beneath a rocky overhang as rocks bounced around the cave floor. Tom clung to his position near the roof as

Nanook leapt across the web towards the great spider.

Arachnid screamed and reared. The razor-sharp teeth on his belly glinted in the bright sunshine. He shot ropes of silk straight at Nanook, who shook them off as if they were flies. There was a flash of Nanook's claws, and an unearthly screech from the spider. Tom gasped. Nanook had slashed into Arachnid's six eyes, blinding the Beast!

"Now, Elenna!" Tom roared. "Save Silver! I'll cut Etta free!"

The giant spider shrieked and thumped at the cave walls with his legs. Nanook growled and beat her chest. In the chaos, Elenna dashed from her rocky hiding place and leapt across the web, bouncing and staggering on its sticky threads. With her knife she slashed at the silk

that bound the wolf, then dragged Silver away from the web's deadly embrace to the safety of the cave floor.

"Silver," Elenna sobbed, throwing her arms around the wolf's shaggy neck as he gently licked her arm. "I'm so glad you're safe."

Tom whistled for Storm, who cantered from beneath the overhang. Then he dropped onto the stallion's back. Storm whinnied in triumph.

"While there's blood in my veins, we can do this!" Tom shouted, holding his sword high. He turned Storm towards Etta and dug his heels into the stallion's sides.

Storm cantered across the uneven rocks, bounding over the cracks and crevasses. The cave was shaking as the two great Beasts fought. Arachnid was lunging and snapping, fighting with all eight legs, as Nanook swiped the air with her fearsome claws.

Tom threw himself from the saddle and scrambled across to Etta. The cave walls groaned. Cracks appeared, snaking from the floor to the roof as pebbles rained down from the ceiling. They didn't have much time. The woman was bound so tightly that all Tom could see was a pair of terrified eyes staring out at him. How could he free her without cutting her with his sword?

Trusting to the power of his gauntlets to help him, Tom let his sword fly. His aim felt truer than it had ever been. *Slash! Slash!*

"Thank you, oh thank you," Etta sobbed as the web fell away from her. “How can I repay you? How—”

“Tom!” Elenna screamed. “The roof is falling in!”

“Take the animals to safety, Elenna!” he shouted. “Go with my friend,” he said to Etta. “She will keep you safe.”

“But what are you going to do?” stammered Etta.

“Fight the Beast,” Tom said grimly.

Elenna grabbed Etta by the hand and ran for the fresh hole in the cave wall created by Nanook’s entrance. Silver raced at her side. The ground shuddered as the Beasts swayed and struck at one another. Even without sight, Arachnid was matching Nanook blow for blow. The spider’s razor-like teeth tore into Nanook’s flesh, scattering red blood on the rocks. *What if Nanook was unable to defeat*

this monster? Tom wondered. *If it was too much for a great Beast of Avantia, then what chance did he have?*

But Tom knew that every time he faltered, Aduro would be lowered even closer to Malvel's pit of tar. He had to stay strong, for Aduro's sake! If he could just get back to that stalactite and tear it free…

Tom leapt onto Storm. Bending low over the stallion's neck, he galloped over to the stalactite he had tried to break away from the cave roof. Storm skidded to a halt as Tom scrambled to his feet on the stallion's broad back. He tensed his muscles and once more felt the golden leg armour fill his legs with strength. Then he jumped.

Soaring over the heads of the fighting Beasts, Tom landed hard on the stalactite, the golden gauntlets helping him to grip. The stalactite shuddered, jarred by the impact. Tom could see a crack forming where the calcite spear joined the roof. He drew his sword and hacked at the crack.

"One more blow," Tom panted, striking it again and again. "Just one more..."

There was a groan as the stalactite tore away from the roof and fell – with Tom still clinging to it.

With a crunch, the stalactite plunged into Arachnid's back. The Beast let out a roar of pain. Tom threw himself free as the spider arched his vile body in agony, hurling himself around the cave, trying to get the stalactite out. But every time the Beast struck a wall, the impact drove the stalactite deeper into his flesh.

At last the huge spider gave one final roar and disappeared.

In its place, thousands of tiny spiders skittered madly across the rocks. Arachnid had been defeated!

But Tom had no time to celebrate. A booming noise sounded above him and great chunks of rock began to fall from the walls. Chasms opened at Tom's feet. Everything was collapsing.

"Nanook!" Tom yelled, pulling himself to his feet. "We must get out of here before it's too late!"

The great snow monster roared.

Tom began to run towards the daylight as the mountain caved in.

CHAPTER NINE

STAY STRONG!

Tom hurled himself outside, rocks cascading around him. The whole mountainside seemed to be falling apart. The noise was deafening.

Shocked and bruised, Tom realised that he was standing on the rocky outcrop where Etta had entered the caves. Now a new cave yawned where Nanook had smashed her way inside the mountain, but its mouth was steadily filling with falling rocks.

"This way!" Elenna yelled, grabbing Tom's arm.

But he pulled his arm from Elenna's grasp. "We have to go back," he said. "Nanook is still in there!"

Tom threw himself towards the cave they had just left, lifting his shield above his head for protection. Falling rocks bounced and shuddered against the sturdy wood. The rocks were already piled as high as Tom's shoulders, blocking Nanook's escape.

"It's impossible," Elenna shouted through the noise. "We have to leave, Tom! Etta has gone ahead. I promised we would follow—"

"No!" Tom yelled. "I won't leave Nanook. She helped me!"

He scrabbled at the rocks,

throwing himself repeatedly at them. But it was a hopeless task. Tom could feel his courage failing.

He felt a hand on his shoulder. "I'm sorry, Tom," Elenna said. Silver stood at her side. "You're right. We have to save Nanook."

Storm whinnied and trotted over to nudge Tom on the shoulder. Stroking the stallion's neck, Tom stared at the blocked cave mouth.

"With all of us, we can do it," Tom said firmly.

Tom and Elenna threw themselves at the rocks. They heaved and pulled, pushed and tugged. Silver nosed among the boulders and Storm pounded at the rocks with his hooves. But nothing moved.

Help me, Aduro! Tom thought desperately. He had never needed the good wizard so much. But Aduro was in Malvel's grasp. He couldn't help them now.

Suddenly there was a shimmer in the air behind Elenna. Tom stared, hardly daring to believe his eyes, as Aduro stepped onto the mountainside.

"There is no time for questions," Aduro said, holding up his hand. He looked gaunt, with dark circles beneath his eyes. Tom's heart ached for his friend.

"I have only a few moments before Malvel realises I am missing," Aduro said. "You are doing well, Tom. Better than I could have hoped. Stay strong!"

The wizard raised his hands towards the rocks. He muttered some powerful magic words and there was a blast of white light. The rocks exploded. Storm whinnied in terror and Silver howled. Tom and Elenna fell to the ground and covered their eyes.

When they dared to open them, they saw that the rocks blocking the cave mouth had been blasted to powder. The entrance was clear!

Tom whirled round to thank Aduro. But to his horror, he saw the furious figure of Malvel grabbing the good wizard and dragging him away!

"You think you can defy me, Aduro?" Malvel roared. "I have been too patient with you. The pit of tar awaits!"

"No!" Tom shouted as Malvel's mocking laughter faded and Aduro vanished from sight. What had they done? Was this the end for their friend?

"Oh, Tom," Elenna choked. "Poor Aduro!"

They heard heavy footsteps. Nanook stepped out of the cave, blinking in the daylight. She was covered in dust, but otherwise looked as powerful as ever.

"Nanook!" Tom cried, overwhelmed with relief. "You're safe!"

The great Beast growled softly. She stretched out a massive white paw and laid it gently on Tom's head. Awestruck, Tom gazed into her fierce blue eyes.

The Beast threw out her chest and roared at the sky. Then she turned and walked away from Tom and his friends, climbing the mountainside with ease and grace – back to the snowy lands of the north.

Tom closed his eyes. Then he opened them again and stared at Elenna. She was smiling.

"Well done," she said. "You've conquered another Beast! Arachnid was truly evil."

Tom stroked his gleaming golden armour. Helmet, chainmail, breastplate, leg armour and now the gauntlets. There was just one piece left – and one more Beast to fight. He had to stay strong. That glimpse of Malvel made Tom even more determined to rescue his friend before something awful could happen. With his companions, he would complete his Quest. And Malvel's power over Aduro would be broken.

Then came a familiar sound, which felt like a shard of ice in Tom's heart.

Malvel's laughter boomed around the broken mountainside. It bounced off the rocks and crevasses. Tom felt it wrap around him like Arachnid's deadly web.

"So!" boomed the evil wizard's voice. "You think you will defeat me? Your stupidity today nearly cost the life of one of Avantia's protectors. Is this Quest worth it?" His voice lowered to a whisper. *"Is it truly worth it?"*

Tom lifted his head. "While there's blood in my veins, I will defeat you, Malvel!" he shouted. He pulled his sword from its scabbard and pointed it to the sky. "We go to meet the final Beast!"

Join Tom on the next stage of the Beast Quest

Meet

TRILLION THE THREE-HEADED LION

Can Tom and Elenna collect the golden armour and free Avantia?

PROLOGUE

The sun was setting over the central plains of Avantia. Tagus the horse-man, good Beast and protector of the land, nodded his head contentedly. All was peaceful, as it had been ever since Tom had freed him from the evil curse of Malvel the Dark Wizard.

It was time to rest. Tagus stamped a heavy hoof and turned to look at the cattle in the distance. A strange shape had appeared on an outcrop of rock on the far horizon, the sun behind it. Some kind of large animal was watching the herd.

A predator!

Tagus trotted forward warily, keeping to the cover of rocks and trees as he approached the creature. At last he was close enough to see clearly.

It was a huge three-headed lion, the sunlight shining on its thick golden fur and the shaggy manes that hung from its three heads. Six eyes burned with a wicked emerald light as it gazed down at the cattle, and its lips were drawn back to reveal fearsome, slavering teeth.

Tagus knew immediately that this was an evil Beast, sent by Malvel to cause mayhem. Instinct told him that he must confront the lion and do all in his power to destroy it. He eyed the huge paws, each one the size of his own head and studded with long, razor-sharp claws. Then, with a fierce cry, he galloped out of cover, drawing his sword as he pounded towards the lion.

The three heads turned and the three mouths bellowed with anger and hatred. The lion pounced from its position on the rock, filling the whole sky as it came crashing down on Tagus. The horse-man's sword spun from his hand as the two mighty Beasts rolled across the ground.

Tagus fought hard, kicking with his hooves and gripping one of the lion's three throats. But the two other heads came snapping at him and he could smell the Beast's foul breath as the three sets of teeth sought to tear his flesh from his bones.

A powerful double blow from Tagus's back legs sent the lion sprawling. Panting, the horse-man got to his feet, but the evil Beast attacked again, jaws snapping, and its terrible weight bore him to the ground. Tagus had never known such strength and savagery before. He could feel deep wounds on his flanks and neck, and sensed his death was near. The lion pinned him to the ground, its back arching as the three heads lifted and let out deafening, triumphant roars.

Tagus struggled valiantly, but he was already too weak to break free. The heads bent down now, hungry eyes glowing, jaws snapping and ready to sink into Tagus's flesh…

Suddenly an arrow came shooting out of nowhere, the sharp point sinking deep into one of the lion's paws.

The monster let out a roar of anger and leapt back, its great body trembling with rage. Tagus tried to get up, but he was too badly wounded.

While one of the lion's heads tore at the arrow, the other two were turning, their blazing eyes searching for the archer. A second arrow hissed, narrowly missing one of the heads. With an ear-splitting roar, the lion took off, bounding away towards the darkening plains.

Gasping with relief, Tagus looked up.

Two familiar shapes stood on the high horizon: a boy whose golden armour shone in the light of the setting sun, and a girl with another arrow already fitted to her bow. A horse and a wolf stood poised on the rocky outcrop behind them.

CHAPTER ONE

THE WOUNDED BEAST

"Tagus is hurt!" Tom cried, scrambling onto his horse. "Quickly, Storm!"

Elenna leapt up behind Tom. The black stallion neighed and reared, his hooves striking the air, before he set off at a gallop. Tom and Elenna clung grimly to his back, with Elenna's loyal wolf Silver close behind.

They came down off the stony crag and sped across the plains to where the injured horse-man lay. Tagus was still struggling to get to his feet, but his battle with the monstrous three-headed lion had left him weak and helpless.

Tom peered into the distance. The evil Beast had fled, leaving no trace. There would be time enough to deal with Malvel's monster later. Right now they had to help Tagus.

"That lion would have killed Tagus if it wasn't for your arrows," Tom shouted to Elenna as they galloped along.

"It has to be one of Malvel's evil Beasts,"

Elenna replied, concern in her voice. "Do you think it's the guardian of the golden boots?"

"It must be," Tom said. "This is Malvel's final challenge – and when we win, I will have every piece of the missing golden armour."

The magical armour, the most precious relic in the kingdom, had been scattered throughout Avantia by the Dark Wizard. Each piece was watched over by a fearsome Beast under Malvel's thrall. So far, Tom had defeated five Beasts and collected the helmet, chainmail, breastplate, gauntlets and leg armour. Each piece had given him new powers. Now only the boots were missing.

But Malvel had held back his most deadly Beast until last! The huge, savage creature had defeated Tagus – how could he and Elenna stand up to such a monster, even with the help of his magical shield and his golden armour?

Tom gritted his teeth. Whatever the outcome, he would find that Beast and do battle with it. All of Avantia was relying on him.

They came to where Tagus lay. The foul, musky scent of the three-headed lion hung thickly in the air. The two friends leapt down from Storm's back and ran to Tagus. His wounds were deep and bloody, showing the dreadful marks of claws and razor-sharp fangs.

"Careful!" Tom said, as Tagus fought to get to his feet. "We'll help you. Slowly now!" The Beast could not understand human speech, but Tagus would know that they meant to help.

Tom and Elenna did their best to support the horse-man as he struggled to stand. Storm came close, whinnying gently and bowing his head so that Tagus could pull himself up.

At last the wounded horse-man was upright, his arm across Storm's neck, the stallion pressing close so that Tagus would not fall. Silver prowled around them, his sharp eyes alert for danger.

"He needs to rest and recover," Elenna said, "but he won't be able to travel far." She looked at Tom. "What should we do?"

Tom pointed back towards the outcrop. The rock-face curved inwards, forming a natural place of shelter.

"If we can get him there, he should be hidden from danger while we deal with the lion," Tom replied. He turned to the horse-man.

"Come with us," he said, pointing to the outcrop. "You'll be safe there."

Tagus nodded, his face twisted with pain. Very slowly, and with Storm at his side, he began to limp forwards.

Tom and Elenna walked at Tagus's other side, ready to help if the good Beast faltered.

"He's badly hurt," Elenna said in a low voice. "He won't be able to help us against the lion."

Tom nodded grimly. In their Quest for the golden armour they had been aided by the good Beasts of Avantia, but it seemed that this final test would have to be completed alone.

Then the sound of cruel laughter echoed across the plains.

"Malvel!" Tom gasped, his fingers closing on the hilt of his sword.

A dark swirl, like a small whirlwind, had appeared in the sky. When it cleared, the Dark Wizard was standing in front of them, his eyes flashing.

Tom drew his blade.

"Don't try to strike me," Malvel sneered. "You know you can do me no harm!" He laughed again and stretched out a hand towards them, his long, thin fingers like claws. "You are doomed. Your Quest is at an end! Tagus will die and you will fall to the power of Trillion – the most savage and deadly Beast you have ever encountered!"

"We're not scared of you or the Beasts you keep under your spells!" Elenna shouted. "You're the one who should be scared!"

"I?" Malvel laughed. "Scared of you? No, child, I feel no fear. But fear is coming for you – can you not hear it? Padding this way on four mighty paws? Listen carefully now..."

"You're a coward," Tom shouted.

Malvel's face twisted with rage. "I will make you one oath, boy," he spat. "I promise you pain and destruction if you dare to fight Trillion. He is more dangerous than you could ever imagine!" His eyes glowed. "And when you lie dying, I will be there – and my face will be the last thing you will ever see!"

Then the dark whirlwind rose again, while the sky shook to the awful noise of the wizard's laughter.

Malvel was gone.

Tom turned to Elenna. "Aduro wasn't with

him this time," he said.

Previously, Malvel had shown them horrible visions of their friend and adviser, the good wizard Aduro, bound and helpless above a pit of boiling tar. Tom knew that the only way to save Aduro was by collecting each piece of the golden armour and finishing the Quest.

"What do you think that means?" Elenna asked. "Has Malvel done something terrible to him?"

"I don't know," Tom replied, a fierce determination in his voice. "But when this Quest is over, I will make Malvel pay for all his wickedness."

He gazed at the plains. Somewhere out there Trillion was guarding the golden boots. Tom raised his sword to the sky.

"Whatever it takes!" he called out. "I will find you, Trillion! I will complete my Quest!"

Follow this Quest to the end in TRILLION THE THREE-HEADED LION.

Win an exclusive
Beast Quest T-shirt and goody bag!

Tom has battled many fearsome Beasts and we want to know which one is your favourite! Send us a drawing or painting of your favourite Beast and tell us in 30 words why you think it's the best.

Each month we will select **three** winners to receive a Beast Quest T-shirt and goody bag!

Send your entry on a postcard to
BEAST QUEST COMPETITION
Orchard Books, 338 Euston Road, London NW1 3BH.

Australian readers should email:
childrens.books@hachette.com.au

New Zealand readers should write to:
Beast Quest Competition, PO Box 3255, Shortland St, Auckland 1140, NZ or email: childrensbooks@hachette.co.nz

Don't forget to include your name and address.
Only one entry per child.

Good luck!